Jo makes cute faces on her toes.
Jo gave names to her five toes.
Jo's toes are Bo, Ho, Moe, Poe, and Wo.

2

Jo ties bows on her toes.
Jo's toes pose with the bows.

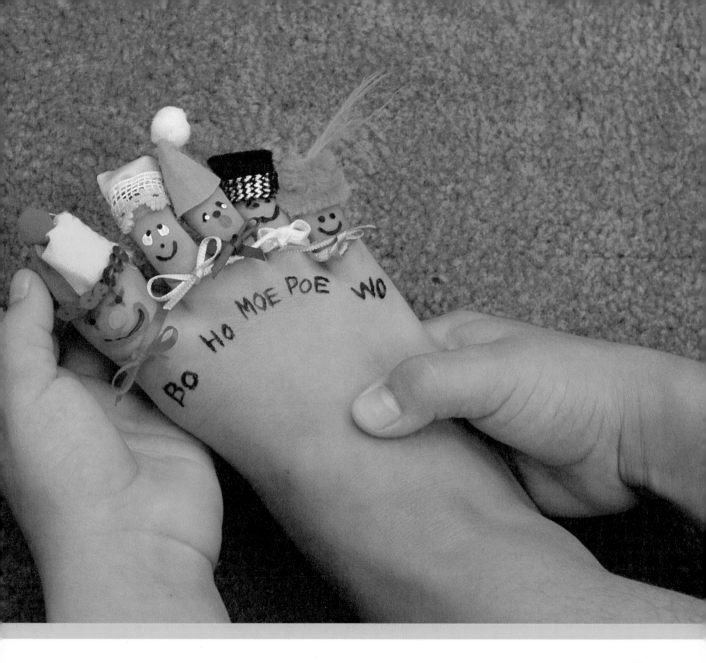

Jo's toes like the nice hats.
Is Moe's hat like a cone?

3

4

Bo is Jo's big toe.
Can Bo poke Jo's nose?

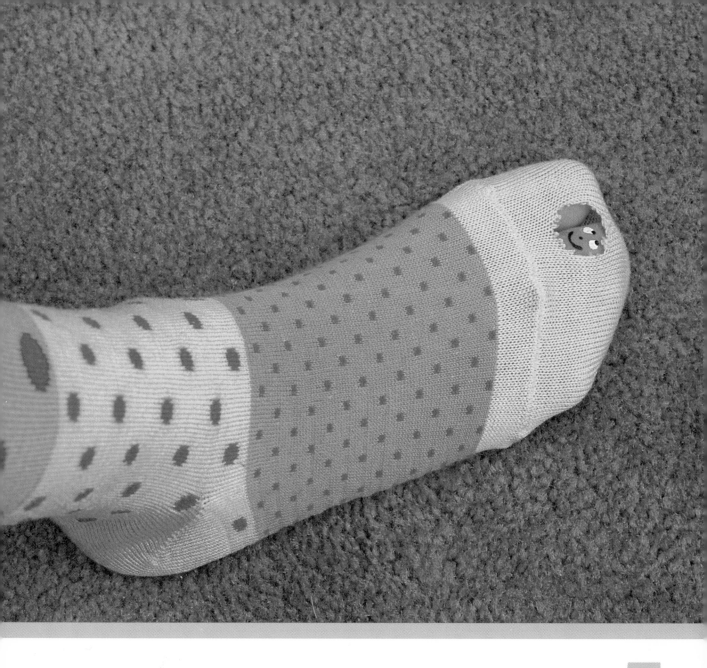

Bo, Moe, Poe, and Wo hide from Jo.
Can you see Ho's nose in the hole?

5

6

The soap makes suds and foam.
Jo's toes have fun in the tub.

Jo ties a rope to her toes.
Jo's toes tug the rope and tow the boat.

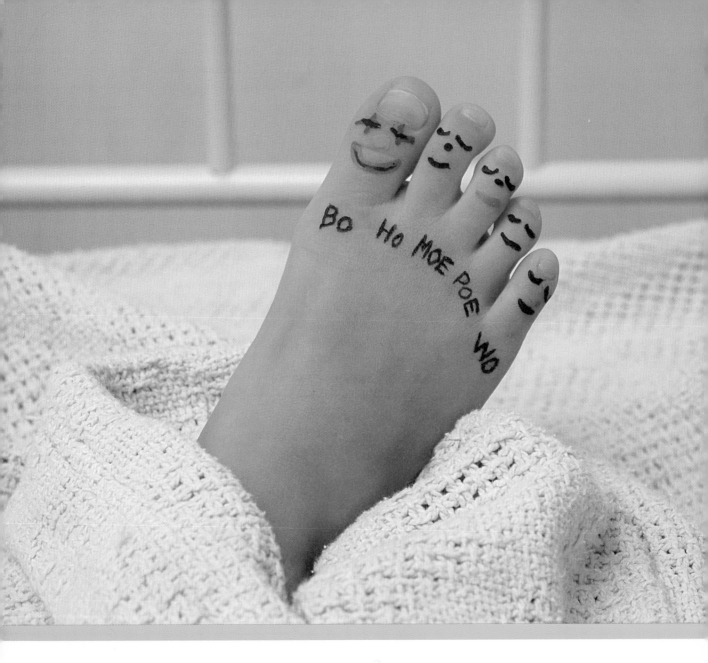

8 It is time for Jo to take a nap.
Bo, Ho, Moe, Poe, and Wo doze too!